The All Aboard Reading series is especially designed for beginning readers. Written by noted authors and illustrated in full color, these are books that children really want to read—books to excite their imagination, expand their interests, make them laugh, and support their feelings. With fiction and nonfiction stories that are high interest and curriculum-related, All Aboard Reading books offer something for every young reader. And with four different reading levels, the All Aboard Reading series lets you choose which books are most appropriate for your children and their growing abilities.

Picture Readers

Picture Readers have super-simple texts, with many nouns appearing as rebus pictures. At the end of each book are 24 flash cards—on one side is a rebus picture; on the other side is the written-out word.

Station Stop 1

Station Stop 1 books are best for children who have just begun to read. Simple words and big type make these early reading experiences more comfortable. Picture clues help children to figure out the words on the page. Lots of repetition throughout the text helps children to predict the next word or phrase—an essential step in developing word recognition.

Station Stop 2

Station Stop 2 books are written specifically for children who are reading with help. Short sentences make it easier for early readers to understand what they are reading. Simple plots and simple dialogue help children with reading comprehension.

Station Stop 3

Station Stop 3 books are perfect for children who are reading alone. With longer text and harder words, these books appeal to children who have mastered basic reading skills. More complex stories captivate children who are ready for more challenging books.

In addition to All Aboard Reading books, look for All Aboard Math Readers™ (fiction stories that teach math concepts children are learning in school); All Aboard Science Readers™ (nonfiction books that explore the most fascinating science topics in age-appropriate language); and All Aboard Poetry Readers™ (funny, rhyming poems for readers of all levels).

All Aboard for happy reading!

Visit www.strawberryshortcake.com to join the Friendship Club and redeem your Strawberry Shortcake Berry Points for "berry" fun stuff!

Strawberry Shortcake™ © 2005 by Those Characters From Cleveland, Inc. Used under license by Penguin Young Readers Group. All rights reserved. Published by Grosset & Dunlap, a division of Penguin Young Readers Group, 345 Hudson Street, New York, New York 10014. ALL ABOARD READING and GROSSET & DUNLAP are trademarks of Penguin Group (USA) Inc. Printed in the U.S.A.

Library of Congress Cataloging-in-Publication Data

Curry, Kelli.
 Strawberry Shortcake and the butterfly garden / by Kelli Curry ; illustrated by Artful Doodlers.
    p. cm. — (All aboard reading. Station stop 1)
 "Strawberry Shortcake."
 Summary: Strawberry Shortcake and her friends visit a butterfly garden.
 ISBN 0-448-43643-4 (pbk.)
 [1. Butterflies—Fiction. 2. Butterfly gardens—Fiction.] I. Artful Doodlers. II. Title. III. Series.
 PZ7.C9363St 2005
 [E]—dc22

                                                           2004006761

 ISBN 0-448-43643-4   10 9 8 7 6 5 4 3 2 1

Strawberry Shortcake and the Butterfly Garden

By Kelli Curry
Illustrated by Artful Doodlers

Grosset & Dunlap • New York

Strawberry Shortcake
loves butterflies
berry much!

She can't wait to see
lots of butterflies
at the Butterfly Garden.

The Butterfly Garden is
a special home for butterflies.

It has everything they need—
food, water, sun, and flowers.
It helps keep them safe.

Butterflies love flowers.

8

So does Orange Blossom!

Butterflies love
the colors red and pink.

So does Strawberry Shortcake!

Butterflies have
berry pretty wings.
Ginger Snap wishes
she could touch one.

12

But she doesn't.
Touching a butterfly
can hurt it.
Ginger Snap knows
she should only look
at butterflies.

13

The kids are hungry.
They eat their snacks.

The butterflies are hungry, too.

What do they eat?

Flower juice!

When it is time to go,
Angel Cake reminds
Huckleberry Pie
to close the door.
That will keep the butterflies
safe in their home.

Huck sees

a berry pretty butterfly.

He stops to look at it.

He forgets to close the door.

The butterfly flies
up, up,
up in the air.

The kids have to catch
the butterfly.
But how?

Strawberry Shortcake
has an idea!

The kids pick lots of flowers—
lots of red and pink flowers.

They put the flowers
on Strawberry Shortcake's hat.

Strawberry Shortcake
sits berry still.
She is berry quiet.

Here comes the butterfly!

Huck uses a net
to catch the butterfly.

Got it!

Hooray!

Strawberry Shortcake
and her pals
take the butterfly back
to its home.
Berry good job, everybody!

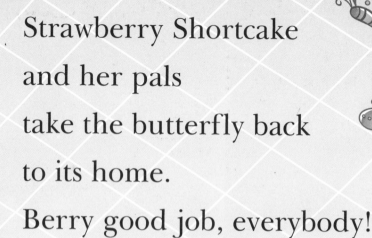